I0589090

The

Hermit

Bookstore

Also by Linda Westphal

The Medium

The
Hermit
Bookstore

a novella

Linda Westphal

LindaWestphal.com

The Hermit Bookstore

Copyright © 2015 by Linda Westphal

Cover photograph copyright © by Bill Alber,
Flickr: BillsExplorations

The characters and events in this book are fictitious. Any
similarity to real persons, living or dead, is coincidental and
not intended by the author.

All rights reserved. In accordance with the U.S. Copyright
Act of 1976, the scanning, uploading, and electronic
sharing of any part of this book without the permission of
the author is unlawful piracy and theft of the author's
intellectual property. If you would like to use material from
this book (other than for review purposes), prior written
permission must be obtained by contacting the author.

Paperback v1.0
ISBN-10: 0986098337
ISBN-13: 978-0-9860983-3-8

A heartfelt thanks to Jonathan and Michael C.

The

Hermit

Bookstore

Unexplained events happen every day.

This is just one event.

Mary June

Wednesday, April 23, 2014

A fine misty rain fell on the small northern California town of Lotus as Mary June Shaw jogged the curves of Lotus Road. She had considered blaming the seasonal mix of dewy clouds and early morning sunlight outside her bedroom window for her inability to sleep, but her instincts hinted at something else—something important she had to do today. Whatever it was, it had coaxed her out of bed at dawn on her day off as marketing director at Rivers Winery.

Lotus, population 295, had not always been a small, quiet town. More than 165 years ago, when gold was discovered here, the nearby American River was overrun within a few months by men from all over the world who dreamed of finding their fortunes.

Mary June slowed her pace, took in the view, and wondered what her little town may have been like during the California gold rush. She imagined makeshift camps along the river that offered the essentials—a doctor, a blacksmith, a sleeping lodge, a food kitchen, a tavern, mail services, and other services a man was willing to trade for a little gold.

Surely, she thought, the scene was nothing like today's quiet picturesque destination that was abandoned most of the year, except in the summer when families and groups dropped in for the thrill of whitewater rafting on the river.

Her gait changed to a fast walk as she approached the Uniontown Cemetery and focused on her breathing—in and out, in and out, in and out. In the distance she could see the tiny old brick post office, built in 1881, and just beyond it a farmhouse about the same age.

It wasn't until she reached the front of the old post office that she saw a light in the downstairs window of the farmhouse—a house that was supposed to be vacant. She stood still, barely breathing, and narrowed her eyes to get a better look. "Oh my God," she whispered. Her heart pounded in her chest. *Someone's in the house!*

Mary June crossed the street and approached cautiously, taking a second look at a large wooden sign hanging from a post in front of the house. She was sure it had not been there yesterday. Then she noticed the For Sale sign that had been posted at the edge of the yard, near the road, was gone.

She shifted her weight to her right leg and leaned forward until she could see the front of the new sign, which hung from two large metal hooks that were attached to a wooden post. She read the words carved into the wood—The Hermit Bookstore. A carved drawing next to the name featured a cloaked man with a brightly lit lantern in one hand and a walking stick in the other.

She walked up to the farmhouse and through a side window saw an older woman, dressed in a long rainbow-patterned skirt and a loose white blouse, placing books on a bookshelf that stood higher than her five-foot frame. She watched the woman for a few minutes, then moved toward the front of the house, walked up the stairs, and crossed the front porch. Without thinking, she knocked on the door.

Before she finished knocking, the woman she had been watching—with her hippie-like clothes, long blonde wavy hair, and sparkling blue eyes that reminded Mary June of the American River on a bright sunny day—opened the door.

"Hello! You're my first customer today," said the stranger on the other side of the threshold. She held the door open for Mary June.

It took Mary June a moment to react. The scene behind the woman was not what she had expected. On the floor, running down the middle of the parlor, lay a faded Persian rug with various shades of gold that matched the honey-colored oak floor and wood trim. The welcoming sight pulled her eyes a good twenty feet into the room to a round antique table full of books at the opposite end of the rug. Mary June's nose twitched as she caught a whiff of sweet lilacs, old books, and worn furniture. "Umm, hi," she finally managed to say.

She thought she heard the woman giggle softly in her throat, but the mature face looking back at her only offered a pleasant smile. As she studied the stranger's face (her shockingly-white skin and crow's-feet just starting to form at the corners of her eyes), she could not recall if they had ever met. The woman was a stranger but she didn't feel like a stranger. Mary June wasn't at all uncomfortable when the woman caught and held her gaze for a long minute, as if she was looking inside her, watching her life's story.

"This is Feather," the woman said, breaking the connection and referring to the furry-faced, butt-wagging mutt at her feet. "And I'm Jolene. Jolene Fields. Welcome to The Hermit Bookstore." She opened the door wider and attached a hook on the door to an eye latch on the wall.

Mary June's feet remained planted on the front porch, her upper body stretched halfway in the door. She looked wide-eyed at the old farmhouse parlor and the room beyond it, which was once the dining room. Tall, wooden bookshelves stood like soldiers in vertical rows to the left and right of the Persian rug, and a creamy white marble fireplace stood against the wall on her right.

She had never seen the farmhouse look so good; somehow, it looked fifty years younger. The floors, polished back to life, glowed as sunlight from the windows hit the planks. The matching oak molding throughout the two rooms appeared almost new. The farmhouse had been transformed into a fabulous bookstore with row after row of six-foot-high shelves packed with books. The only thing out of place was a small box of unpacked books in front of a shelf where Jolene was standing.

Less than twenty-four hours ago the building had been a cold, abandoned farmhouse. But now, with its warm and inviting atmosphere, a person might think it had been there for years. It hardly seemed possible that someone could pull it together so quickly, and without any gossip about it at Sutter Diner.

"Come on in, darlin'. Look around if you'd like."

Mary June watched Jolene pull books from the box and place them on the shelf marked History. "Did the owners sell the farmhouse?" she asked, stepping inside the room.

"I'm just renting it temporarily."

Mary June frowned, wondering why anyone would go to so much trouble for a temporary bookstore. The thought faded away as soon as she reached the round antique table at the end of the rug. A small metal sign that read Shopkeeper's Monthly Picks sat on top of a stack of books. She walked slowly around the table, scanning the book titles. The books included a mix of adult and children's classics, a few New York Times bestsellers, and a number of titles she didn't recognize. One book in particular stood out—a hardcover novel with a plantation house and live oak trees on the front cover.

"Can I help you find something?"

Startled, Mary June looked up to see Jolene's kind, blue eyes. Jolene caught and held her gaze again, then turned and appeared to be searching for a book on the shelf behind her.

"What do you like to read? Fiction or nonfiction?" Jolene asked, finally pulling the book she was looking for from the shelf.

"This looks interesting," Mary June said. She turned the book in her hand so Jolene could see the front cover.

"Well, bless your heart. Are you a Southern girl, too?"

Mary June blushed and averted her eyes. "I was."

"My dear, once a Southern girl, always a Southern girl."

Mary June nodded and smiled. She may have left rural Georgia more than nine years ago, but she still felt like a Southern girl at heart.

"Where's your family from, dear?" Jolene asked.

"Mama's family is from Alabama, Daddy's from Mississippi."

"Yes indeed. You come from good Southern roots. When did you come to California, sugar?"

Mary June hesitated. She wasn't sure she wanted to talk to a stranger about her troubled family history. "I've been here awhile." Turning her shoulder as she pulled her attention back to the table, she hoped Jolene would get the hint that she had shared enough.

"Here, take this." Jolene held up the book Mary June had seen her take from the shelf. "Consider it a gift from one Southern girl to another."

Her eyes smiled.

Mary June took the book and read the title—
Travels with Charley. It sounded somewhat familiar.
Then she noticed the author's name, John Steinbeck.
Of course, she thought, *the author of* Of Mice and Men
and The Grapes of Wrath.

"Thank you," she said, giving Jolene a grateful
smile. "How much do I owe you for this one?" She
held up the Southern novel she had found on the
table.

Jolene checked the back cover. "Six dollars
and fifty cents should cover it. Would you like a bag
for your books?"

"No. I live around the corner. I can carry
them." Mary June pulled a ten-dollar bill from the
zippered pocket of her jogging jacket and handed it to
Jolene.

Jolene rang up the sale and returned the
change. "I'm glad you stopped by to say hello, Mary
June." Jolene stared purposefully as she spoke. "Come
back soon and let me know what you think of
Steinbeck's book."

As Mary June walked to her apartment,
replaying the strange encounter with Jolene in her
mind, she wondered if the bookstore was the reason

she couldn't sleep this morning. How did Jolene know she was at the front door? How did she know her name? Mary June had never mentioned her name. And what about that book? Jolene had intentionally pulled *Travels with Charley* from the shelf for her. However strange the experience had been, it didn't feel creepy. In fact, it felt good, perhaps even . . . necessary. Maybe things would make sense when she started reading it. She picked up her pace and didn't slow until she reached her apartment.

Mario

Wednesday, April 23, 2014

The morning sun had tried to force its way through the window blinds of the law office reception area about an hour ago, but Mario Pico didn't bother getting up to let it in. He liked to work in the dark with only the banker's light on his desk illuminating the room. He had picked up this habit in law school, where he did his best work at night when it was quiet and he was alone.

Mario leaned all the way back in the leather chair at his desk and stretched his arms, causing his fingertips to tap the window blinds behind him. This made him think of the many strained conversations he had had with his secretary, Tracey, about the blinds. She didn't think it mattered if they were closed at night, but to him it was a big deal because he usually arrived and left when it was dark. The mere suggestion that someone could be watching him from the other side of a dark window spooked him, and made it impossible for him to concentrate on his work. He also worried about the contents of the office, not wanting to tempt thieves who may be lurking around the neighborhood. "Just close them when you leave; it solves a number of issues," he reminded Tracey at least once a week. Her usual response was an eye roll and the line, "What would I do if I didn't have you to remind me?"

His thoughts drifted to the number of hours he worked and his less-than-perfect love life. At his thirtieth birthday party last week, he had done a pretty good job of deflecting the hazing from his friends about showing up without a date, but he knew what they said was true. Last year he wanted to give Katie what she wanted—marriage—but he didn't feel ready for it. In retrospect, he didn't blame her for wanting to end the relationship. In fact her ability to move forward once she had made a decision about what she wanted was one of the characteristics he had admired most about her.

He shook off the chatter in his head and sat up in the chair. It was still early, just after eight in the morning. Tracey would be in soon. He opened his calendar on his laptop. Except for a court appearance in Sacramento at 3:30 p.m., his day was clear. He reached for a large file on the table next to his desk and began reviewing his notes.

About eleven, he closed the file and reached for his suit jacket that hung on the coat rack near the door.

"I'm going out for a while," he said to Tracey,

who sat at her desk in the reception area. "Can I get you anything?"

"I know it's hard to believe, but"—she gazed up at him sheepishly from the top of her reading glasses—"I didn't have time this morning to pack a lunch. If it's not too much trouble, I'd love a turkey Lunch Box from Sutter Diner."

"You got it." He reached for the door and closed it behind him.

It was too early for lunch, so he decided to take a ride around the curves of Highway 49. When he felt restless, he drove. Anywhere. Driving helped him think.

He slid into the seat of his five-year-old Porsche Carrera and put the key in the ignition. As he drove, his mind walked through each area of his life—his small, one-man law firm was doing surprisingly well, thanks to a few new Sacramento clients who did business in El Dorado County; he was building a new home on the land his grandfather had willed him when he died; his love life was pathetic, true, but he didn't have any trouble getting a date when he needed one. Overall, he had little to complain about. So why, then, did he feel restless about his love life? Unable to explain what he was feeling, he pushed the thoughts away and hoped the feeling would follow.

Highway 49 is a sleepy rural road most of the time, but especially this time of day on a Wednesday. The road appeared more narrow than it had been two weeks ago, probably on account of recent spring rains and the thick vegetation that now lined the road. The cherry trees, in full bloom, threw a thick sweet perfume into the air. And the green grassy hills above the road gleamed in the morning sunshine. Around another curve, a Sierra Nevada Foothills winery paraded neat rows of manicured grape vines with clumps of shiny new leaves.

Mario slowed as he approached a T-intersection with a stoplight. Two gas stations, one with a convenience store, occupied the corners of the wide intersection. He continued on Highway 49 toward Placerville, nearly slowing to a crawl as he drove through a business district that was about a block long. Merchants had moved some of their goods outside on the sidewalk to encourage stopping, browsing, and hopefully a little buying.

Less than an hour later Mario merged onto Lotus Road and headed for Sutter Diner in the center of town. As he passed the historic post office, he noticed a large wooden sign in front of the Spencer-Johnson farmhouse. He was sure he had seen a cheap, rusty For Sale sign posted at the edge of the front yard near the road yesterday. He braked and pulled into the driveway, and read the new sign by the walkway that lead to the front porch—The Hermit Bookstore. "What the—"? he said to himself. He shut off the Carrera and made his way up the porch stairs and through the open doorway.

Between the parlor and the former dining room stood solid oak colonnades with a single fluted square pillar on each side, most likely installed during a remodel in the 1920s. The left side of the wood frame that separated the two rooms glowed as the mid-day light flooded in through the windows and doorway. Mario gaped at the warm, beautiful sight. This wasn't the old, dirty farmhouse he had toured with the owner a few months ago. His eyes moved toward a stack of vintage-looking books on top of the right-side colonnade, which was also a built-in bookcase with glass-front doors. The spines of the books were torn, cracked, and faded—one torn so badly it was nearly gone. He was a collector of vintage books, in love with their finely sewn pages, yellowed paper, and the smell (ahh, the smell).

As he got closer he spotted a pair of antique spectacles on top of the stack of books, and then the book titles—*The Story Girl* by L. M. Montgomery, *Up From Slavery* by Booker T. Washington, and *The Star Rover* by Jack London. A small twinge of bliss emptied into his chest at the thought of having a used bookstore in town. He loved getting lost in bookstores, especially used bookstores. This was exactly what Lotus needed.

He was immediately pulled toward the Travel section and started to browse the shelves. Barely a minute had passed when a woman's voice behind him caused him to leap forward slightly. "You'll want to buy a plane ticket to Italy after reading that book," she said. He turned to see the face of an older woman with kind, bright eyes, a kid-like smile, and wavy hair just below her shoulders. He thought he knew everyone in Lotus, but he didn't know her.

"Well, that wouldn't be such a bad thing," he said, playing along. The woman grinned and searched his eyes with a long stare.

"I'm Jolene Fields, the owner of this bookstore. Let me know if you need help finding anything." Mario detected a Southern accent.

"Thank you. By the way, when did you open? I don't remember seeing your sign out front yesterday."

"I opened this morning. In fact, I met a very sweet woman earlier . . . Mary June." Mario observed how she moved away from his question.

"Yes, I know Mary June," he said, glancing around the store again, impressed. "I don't know how you did it, but the place looks great. It's nice to have a used bookstore in town." When he turned back to address her, she was gone. She had moved to the end of the aisle and appeared to be consumed with a task in the Classics section. He shrugged it off and went back to scanning the books in front of him.

"Are you an H. G. Wells fan?"

This time his entire body jerked forward. Jolene was standing behind him again. *How does she do that?*

"H. G. Wells?" he replied. "Sure, I guess. I read a few of his books years ago."

"Did you know that of all the books he wrote, this was his favorite?" She handed him *Kipps.*

He looked at the front and back covers. "Is that so. I don't remember reading this one. What's it about?"

"Most people describe it as a rags-to-riches story, but I think it's about understanding life. The main character inherits money and has to adjust to a new way of life. His experiences help him discover his true self."

A rags-to-riches story wasn't something Mario would normally pick up and read, but it was Wells's favorite book and that alone intrigued him. "How can

16

I pass up H. G. Wells's favorite book? I'll take it, along with this book." He handed her a book about northern Italy.

As Jolene rang up the sale, he could feel her glances. He looked up and smiled as he locked eyes with her. He was just as inquisitive about her as she was about him. And then she winked, and a look of clarity crossed her face. "When I'm feeling restless," she said in a matter-of-fact way, "there's nothing like escaping into a book, don't you think?" He pulled a twenty-dollar bill from his wallet, met her eyes again, and then blinked. Had his restlessness gotten so bad that it now showed in his face and body language?

Jolene handed him a cloth bag and said, "I placed a bookmark in the Wells book on a page you should read first. Normally I don't recommend skipping around when reading a story, but in this instance, it's okay."

What an odd woman, Mario thought as he started for the door. But there was something about her that he liked.

"Come back anytime," she said, waving. He returned the wave and made his way across the porch and down the stairs to his car.

He checked his watch, then drove toward Sutter Diner. It took about ten minutes to pick up two Lunch Box specials.

When he returned to the office it was nearly 12:30 p.m. Tracey was on the phone, so he set her lunch on the edge of her desk along with a large iced tea. She mouthed the words *thank you* and he replied with a soft nod.

In his office he hung his jacket on the coat rack and sunk into the large leather sofa. Jolene had placed the bookmark about a third of the way into the H. G. Wells book. When he opened it, he was surprised it was in the middle of a chapter. He chuckled, passing it off as another one of her oddities, and started reading the first sentence in the upper left corner.

Elisa

Wednesday, April 23, 2014

Inside the second-floor one-bedroom apartment of Elisa Evans, as her mind shifted from asleep to awake, she thanked the universe for a full night's sleep—her first in more than a week. Her next thought was about Francisco, her boyfriend of nine months. If she opened her eyes and he was somewhere in the apartment, he'd ruin this peaceful moment. *Don't move*, she told herself.

She lay still, eyes shut, and let her other senses tell her what she wanted to know. He wasn't next to her in bed, or in the room, because the smell of automobile grease—the stuff that seeped into his hair when he worked at Tom's Lube & Tube—was absent. There was also no sound of him moving around in the apartment. If he were there she'd know it, because it was important that the world revolve around Francisco.

She remained still a few minutes more, listening for sounds in the other rooms. When she was sure she was alone, she rolled over and opened her eyes. *Dammit.*

On the far side of the room, near the dresser and closet, an explosion of dirty underwear, T-shirts, jeans, socks, and shoes covered the floor and hung off the top of her dresser. She sighed. "Francisco, you're a slob." She closed her eyes again and quietly hoped he had not been in any other room in the apartment.

Twenty minutes later, after a long warm shower, she went to the kitchen only to find that lover boy had also been in there. She filled the tea kettle with water from the tap, set it on the stove burner, and turned on the gas. In front of the toaster on the counter next to the stove, dried breadcrumbs and grape jelly smears were stuck to the counter. She wiped it clean and added dirty dishes from the sink, the counter, and the table to the dishwasher. This was not the life she had imagined for herself. And she was sure it was not what other twenty-four-year-olds were doing.

When she met Francisco almost a year ago (and fell in lust with him immediately), he had more than a few female admirers in town. He was a cook at Sutter Diner, where she had just been hired as a waitress. A month later they were a couple. Two months later he left the diner to work for Tom at the Lube & Tube. Tom let him flex his part-time hours so he could work a few construction jobs during the spring and summer. Francisco dreamed of some day owning his own construction company. The confident sparkle in his eye when he talked about his dream was more than adorable.

Francisco knew what he wanted and how to make it happen. Life had never been like that for Elisa. A part of her had hoped a little of his confidence would rub off on her. But so far, nine months later, it had not.

Elisa added the last dirty plate to the dishwasher and glanced at the clock on the microwave—12:34. She picked up her cell phone and called Tracey.

"Pico Law Office," said a familiar voice.

"Hi. It's me."

"Hi yourself, stranger. Where've you been?"

"Ah, mostly at work. Are you hungry? Have you eaten lunch yet?"

"Mario just pulled up. He picked up a Lunch Box at the diner for me. Lucky for you I like to share."

Elisa laughed. "Well, as a matter of fact, I do feel lucky today. Francisco left early this morning, so I got a little extra sleep." She paused. "No need to share your lunch. I have leftovers in the fridge from last night. Can you get away from the office for a while?"

"It's been slow all morning. I'm sure Mario won't mind answering the phone for an hour. I'll be over in a few minutes."

"Good. See you." Elisa hit the red button on her phone with her left thumb while opening the refrigerator with her right hand.

As long as she remembered to bring food home from the diner, there was always something to eat in the refrigerator. Francisco had a thing about leftovers—he hated them and only ate food that was prepared fresh. If you put anything in front of him that had been made earlier that day or expected him to eat a meal he hadn't finished the day before, it wasn't happening. He wouldn't touch it. Even pizza.

She set a piece of fried chicken and macaroni and cheese from the diner on a plate and laid a paper towel over the top. Three seconds before the microwave buzzed, she heard a knock on the door.

***

It was just before 2:00 p.m. when Tracey left the apartment to return to the office. That gave Elisa about an hour to kill before she had to be at the diner. She wanted to check out the new bookstore in the Spencer-Johnson farmhouse, next to the old post office, which Tracey mentioned during lunch. Mario told her someone had leased the house.

She threw her backpack over her shoulder and picked up the keys on the table. On the other side of the door, she wiggled the doorknob to be sure it had locked when she shut it.

The Spencer-Johnson farmhouse on Lotus Road was just a few blocks from her apartment and next to her favorite gold rush landmark—the old brick post office. She could see the bookstore sign in front of the farmhouse as soon as she passed the post office. It was as big and as new age as Tracey had described it—at least six feet tall, made of solid wood, with The Hermit Bookstore and a drawing of a man with a lantern carved on both sides of the sign. As she pulled into the driveway, she recognized the drawing as The Hermit, the number nine Major Arcana card from the Rider-Waite tarot deck.

She walked up to the sign and ran her hand over the carving. *Beautiful. This took some skill and effort.*

A woman's cheerful voice from the porch startled her. "Hello!"

Elisa looked up to see an older woman with cornflower blue eyes that stood out against her long, mostly blonde hair and pale skin. Elisa smiled and waved. "Hi."

"Come on in, darlin."

"I get in trouble in bookstores," Elisa said as she climbed the porch stairs. "I love to read. And buy books."

"Well, I can handle that kind of trouble. Get yourself in here. I'll make sure you behave."

Elisa took two steps through the doorway and stopped, her mouth wide open. She observed the rows of tall shelves full of books all crammed into a warm and welcoming space. Throughout the two rooms that she could see, comfortable chairs coaxed her inside. Oddly, every item in sight appeared perfectly placed, as if it had been there for some time. Then she remembered the sign. "Your sign out front," she said, hesitating, not sure how to phrase the question. "I like it."

"Why, thank you. A special family friend carved that for the store."

"Is it The Hermit from the tarot deck?"

Jolene chuckled. "Indeed. The Hermit card, number nine, represents someone who has completed a journey and has learned lessons from that journey. Books do the same thing, don't you think? They can help people with lessons they need to work through."

Elisa thought about this for a moment. "Sure. Interesting connection."

"So, my dear, what kind of books do you like to read?"

Elisa looked around at the bookshelves. "Everything. But I especially like a good story."

"Follow me." Jolene led Elisa to a section designated Adult Literary. "Look through here first. Pull anything you think you'll like. I'll look in the Adult Fiction section around the corner."

More than fifteen minutes had passed before Jolene returned with a book. Elisa was sitting on a low step stool, surrounded by a stack of books. "Find anything?" Jolene asked, smiling.

Elisa eyed the books around her. "A few."

"You weren't kidding. You do like books."

"Now you know why I only go into used bookstores. I can't afford my addiction in a new bookstore." They both laughed. "You've got a good selection," Elisa continued. "I can afford four books today." She pointed at the books on her lap.

"Did I mention our buy-four-get-one-free special?"

Elisa's eyebrows shot up. "No!"

"Here," Jolene said, handing Elisa the book in her hand. "If you like stories, you'll like this one. And it's free when you buy those four books."

Elisa looked at the front cover—*Where the Heart Is* by Billie Letts. "Is it a romance?"

"It's about a young girl who leaves her home in Tennessee to travel to California with her boyfriend. But things don't work out with her boyfriend and she moves on and builds a beautiful new life."

Elisa nodded her head. "Sounds like my kind of story."

"Good. Take your time looking around. I'll be at the front desk when you're ready."

Elisa glanced at her watch—2:40. "Rats! I have to go. I have to be at the diner by three."

Elisa scooped up her books and handed them to Jolene.

At the counter, Jolene rang up the books and placed them in a canvas bag imprinted with the bookstore's name and an image of The Hermit. "Thanks for coming in. By the way, I don't think we've been properly introduced. My name is Jolene.

Jolene Fields."

Elisa hung the bag on her shoulder with her backpack and extended her hand. "It was very nice to meet you, Jolene. I'm Elisa Evans."

Jolene held her hand as she said, "I hope you'll be able to start *Where the Heart Is* today. It's charming."

"I will. Thanks, again."

As Elisa drove away from the old farmhouse, she thought about how comfortable she felt with Jolene. That's a good thing, she thought, because she planned to spend a lot of time in her bookstore.

***

Dinner service on Wednesday, the only day the diner served Southern fried chicken, was always energetic. When Elisa arrived for her shift, she walked through the restaurant and said hello to her coworkers as they rushed past her. *Here we go,* she thought. She washed her hands and then secured a bright-white bistro apron around her waist, taking slow deep breaths. A full dining room didn't freak her out like it used to. As long as she could jump into the rhythm in the room—like jumping into a swinging rope when she was a kid—she could handle five tasks at once, collect good tips (customers had no problem tipping well when the food was extra good), and slide through her shift.

She viewed the Sutter Diner crew and its customers as her family and she loved being part of it. Business meetings took place here, friends caught up on each other's lives here, and families came in for dinner together. To Elisa it was magical, but it was probably time for a change. When she followed her college roommate, Tracey, to Lotus last year after graduating from UC Davis, she intended to lay low for only a few months until companies in the area started to hire again in her field. The owners of the diner—Tracey's sister, Lucy, and her husband, Keith—suggested she work for them while she looked for full-time work. She found it hard to believe their conversation had taken place almost a year ago.

At the end of the night, Elisa finished cleaning the dining room and waitress station and said good night to Keith and Lucy. It was almost 10:00 p.m. when she finally climbed into her car.

On the ride home she thought about the families that came in for the fried chicken dinner. She liked to watch them interact. If she could get away with it without being too annoying, she hovered over their tables—filling water glasses and clearing plates—so she could eavesdrop on their conversations. More than anything, she wanted to know how families interacted. Tracey had told her that her curiosity in this subject was her strangest quality. But Tracey grew up in a typical family, so of course she didn't understand.

Before college, Elisa had spent her whole life in Berkeley. She knew the life she had lived represented a life that most kids wish for—a big house on a hill, access to any material item one could ever want, parents who were not divorced, and two siblings. Her parents spent most of their time thinking about their work. Her father focused on construction projects while her mother focused on the family bakery. Ever since Elisa could remember, the weekends, though always full, never included family activities. She and her two brothers were given whatever they needed to entertain themselves. Family gatherings—evening dinners, vacations, weddings, funerals, and other events—were uncomfortable and more than her parents could handle.

When Elisa left home to attend UC Davis, an hour's drive from Berkeley, she saw it as an opportunity to start over and create a family unit that made her feel connected. It was during one of her sociology lectures that her professor confirmed what she had imagined for herself. "Families are not always related," he said. "They are any group of people who want to share their lives with each other."

The owners of the diner, Keith and Lucy, were like older, wiser siblings. Tracey was a kindred spirit, and many of the locals who ate at the diner were like cousins, aunts, uncles, and grandparents. She felt at home in Lotus with these people and the thought of leaving made her stomach tighten. What if she never found a family like this again? In her heart she wanted to stay and hang onto her new family. But in her head she knew she needed to leave in order to get on with her life.

As she pulled into her parking space at the apartment, her cell phone rang. The unexpected sound made her jump. *Francisco* showed on the display. She tapped the phone and heard only loud, party-like noises. "Francisco? Where are you?"

"Elisa?"

"Yes, hi" she said louder. "Where are you?"

"I'm in Davis, at O'Brien's," he yelled back.

O'Brien's was her old hangout when she attended the university. The call didn't surprise her. She figured he was calling to say he would be home late. *Maybe not at all,* she thought, if he was too drunk to drive. "What's going on at O'Brien's?"

"Taylor and Ted, you know, the twins?"

"Yeah."

"This is their last night in town. The crowd here is crazy. Can you come?" Francisco knew she wouldn't make the one-hour drive. Why did he bother asking? It was after 10:00 p.m. and she had just finished a hectic seven-hour shift.

"No. I just got off work. I'm tired." Elisa paused. "I'll see you later?"

"Of course, babe." A crowd cheered behind his voice. "Gotta go."

The noise from Elisa's phone stopped in mid-cheer. "Bye."

Elisa got out of the car and pressed the alarm button on her key chain. She hadn't seen Francisco all day. Lately, their lives moved in different directions and she wondered why they bothered with the relationship. What were they holding on to? Where did she belong? Not here. Not with Francisco.

Inside the apartment, Elisa set her denim backpack with Southwest Aztec designs on the coffee table. It had been her favorite carryall bag in college and, now, as she noticed its age, she wondered why she never got around to buying a real handbag. A book fell out when she set the bag on the table. *Where the Heart Is*, in big bold letters, stared back at her. It was the book she had assured Jolene she would start reading today. It was a strange request, but she figured Jolene was probably just being friendly and trying to get to know people in town.

Elisa picked up the book and read the author's bio on the back cover. She rarely started a book without knowing something about the author. Then she turned to chapter one.

Mary June

Wednesday, April 23, 2014, evening

Before Mary June finished reading the last chapter of *Travels with Charley*, she knew she had to go back to her hometown, Laurel, Georgia. It was time to resolve her bitter feelings about the family lie her father had dropped on her the day before she left.

She laid the book down on the chaise lounge where she was sitting and watched the early evening sun drop below the horizon.

Nine years of living with the secret had been long enough. It had slowly drained energy from her psyche, and she was tired of it. If she was going to do something meaningful with her life, she needed to resolve the past.

She reached for the glass of dark iced tea on the table next to the chaise and took a sip. It was strong and sweet, just the way she liked it, and, she remembered, just the way it was served in every home and at gatherings all over Georgia. She exhaled a long, serious sigh and set the glass down on the table. Whether she was emotionally ready or not, she had to go back to Laurel.

She relaxed her head on the back of the chaise and closed her eyes. A vision of her father appeared, the same casual look on his face that she had seen the morning he told her the truth. It took him less than sixty seconds to explain the nearly nineteen-year family secret, the same amount of time it took her to lose her entire sense of self. To him and Mother the truth was only a terrible embarrassment that was best left in the past. He had rationalized that as long as he and Mother provided a happy home, the truth really didn't matter. *Could he be that naive?* she remembered thinking.

That morning had started out especially hot and steamy, even for a summer day in Georgia. She had been eighteen years old for twenty-seven days. At breakfast her father asked if she wanted to go riding, a morning tradition they had shared since she was five. Her mother and two brothers had never had an interest in the horses, so caring for and riding the family horses were special tasks she shared with her father.

As they rode to the meadow just beyond the wide oak trees where the horses liked to eat chicory flowers and clover blossoms, she felt a twinge of sadness, knowing she'd miss the ritual once she left for Georgia State. They rode in silence until they reached the meadow, about a mile from the house. Then they tied the horses to a broad branch under a shady tree and sat on a blanket at the edge of the meadow. Before she was able to get comfortable, he said, "Mary June, you're an adult now. It's time you knew the truth."

Puzzled, Mary June looked at her father, whose face appeared worried. "About what, Daddy?"

He took a deep breath and got right to the point in his usual lawyer way. He explained that her birth mother was someone other than the person she had called mother for the past eighteen years.

Before her birth he had been having an affair with the family housekeeper, June, a poor biracial girl in her early 20s. When June became pregnant, Mother had agreed to raise the baby as her own.

At first her father's casual bluntness about something so important shocked Mary June, and then she saw red. "How could you have allowed this?" she shouted at him. "How could Mother be okay with raising your illegitimate child?" Mary June didn't wait for his pathetic explanation. She got up from the blanket, wiped tears on her sleeve, and untied her horse.

Her father's voice shifted, as if he was defending a client in the courtroom. "Back then it wasn't uncommon, Mary June. We had your brothers, a family, and my career to protect." Then his voice softened and his eyes settled on the grove of trees on the other side of the meadow. "Besides, everything turned out all right."

Mary June couldn't stand to be near him another minute. She mounted her horse and rode back to the barn. It was the last time she had spoken to him.

The next morning she packed her car with the last few items that meant anything to her and drove away from her family, away from Laurel, and away from Georgia.

She had nowhere to go, having spent her entire life in Georgia. So she drove west until she couldn't drive anymore. Finally she moved into an apartment in Monterey, California.

Two years later, after she had settled into her new life, she eventually summoned the courage to contact June, her birth mother. She found her in Tampa, Florida, and arranged a trip to visit her. The reunion, twenty years after her birth, was as emotional and life changing as Mary June had expected. She discovered that after the birth, June—young, inexperienced, poor, and half black—had been treated poorly by the family, shunned by the community, and forced to leave Laurel. She believed her only option was to leave her baby with her father and never return.

As Mary June thought about her biological mother's experience, the old angry feelings toward her father and the mother who had raised her filled her chest. How could they have treated June so poorly? How could they have taken a child away from its mother?

Now, nine years later, the idea of returning to Georgia pulled at Mary June harder than ever. The need to go back had always been there, but lately it felt as if the whole universe was pushing her to do something.

It was nearly 7:00 p.m. and her belly growled for attention. She had forgotten to eat lunch and it was now time for dinner. She opened the refrigerator, hoping there were enough ingredients to make a salad. She pulled out half a bag of baby spinach leaves, smoked salmon, leftover bacon from breakfast, goat cheese, and three strips of chives. From the pantry, she found olive oil, Modena balsamic vinegar, and salt and pepper.

With her laptop in front of her, she ate the salad along with a piece of toast at the kitchen counter. As she scrolled through the headlines on a popular news site, an e-mail alert caught her eye when it flashed in the upper right-hand corner of the screen:

Delta's Best Deal of the Year – On All Flights to Atlanta. She laughed at the coincidence.

She opened the e-mail and clicked over to the airline's site, then searched for flights from Sacramento to Atlanta. There was no reason to be surprised that she could leave as soon as tomorrow morning if she wanted to, but surprised she was. And the price? Half the normal rate! *Unbelievable*, she thought. *When all roads (or coincidences) lead to Georgia, a girl's gotta go.*

A few minutes later, the e-ticket arrived in her inbox. She looked at it for a while. "Tomorrow's the day," she said out loud.

As she closed her laptop, she felt an inner calm for the first time in nine years.

Elisa

Thursday, April 24, 2014

It was after one in the morning when she stopped for a bathroom break. Francisco still wasn't home. She decided to keep reading until she reached the halfway mark, about seventy-five more pages. So far she loved the story. The main character, Novalee, was doing the best she could not to mess up her life. Smart and observant, she moved from one tragedy to the next, following her instincts and never giving up. Elisa admired that. It was as if Novalee knew there was something good right around the corner; she just had to hang on.

Elisa fell asleep on the couch and woke after seven when the morning sun streaked through the slit in the living room curtains. She looked around the apartment to see if Francisco had come home. He wasn't in the bedroom or the bathroom. She stretched, raising her arms high in the air to lengthen the muscles in her back, shoulders, and neck. Falling asleep on the couch was never a good idea; it didn't take much for her to get a kink in her neck.

She opened the refrigerator and made a mental note to buy food tomorrow on her day off.

For now, she pulled out orange juice and a blueberry muffin, part of the stash that she brought home from the diner last night. As she thought about her day, she realized she had plenty of time to finish the second half of the book before her scheduled three-to-close shift at the diner. She set the orange juice and muffin on the end table next to the lounge chair and opened the book. It was adorable the way Novalee, Lexie, Sister, Forney, and Moses took care of each other. Elisa felt a kinship with Novalee and found it easy to cheer her on as she read each chapter.

When Elisa reached the last chapter, she was still on the couch, propped up against her two favorite pillows. She smiled, admiring how Novalee had been honest with herself about what she wanted and going after it, without hesitation, when the time came. Elisa wanted to do the same with her life. More than ever, she was feeling a push to move on to something else, somewhere else. She quietly thanked Jolene for recommending the book. It was what she needed.

When she pulled into the diner's parking lot at 2:50 p.m., it was nearly full. It was unusual for it to be this busy on a Thursday afternoon. She rushed in the back door and nearly ran into Keith. "Boy am I glad to see you," he said. "Is it three already? We've been like this since eleven. We sure could use your help up front."

"No problem." Elisa set down her backpack and tied an apron around her waist. "I can take care of the customers at the counter, then relieve Ruth in the dining room at three thirty."

"What would I do without you?" he gushed, causing Elisa to blush.

By 9:30 p.m. the place was empty except for George, a CHP officer, at the counter. Keith patted Elisa on the shoulder and said, "Fantastic job tonight, Elisa."

She smiled. Something was up. He'd been overly complimentary all night.

"Let's sit down a few minutes and talk," he said. He rounded the counter and sat on one of the stools.

Elisa poured two cups of decaf coffee and sat on the stool next to Keith. "So, what's on your mind? Is everything okay?"

"Yes, yes, everything is fine. Lucy and I have good news."

Elisa's face brightened. "Really? What?"

"We're opening another diner in Folsom next month." He grinned. "And we're going to need someone to run the place. We hoped it would be you."

Elisa choked on her coffee. "Me?"

"Sure. Why not? Lucy and I think you'd be great. We've enjoyed having you here the past year. We can see you're getting a little restless. Obviously you can handle a lot more than what we've been able to offer you here."

Elisa was shocked and happy at the same time. The change could be what she was waiting for.

"Try it for a year. Lucy and I would consider a partnership, if you're interested."

The offer kept getting better. She was afraid to say anything. If she stayed quiet, it may get even better. She learned a few years ago that when opportunities come without much effort, and fall into place on their own, these are the chance events she needs to pay attention to, because they usually turn out to be exactly what she needs. She sensed that this was one of those moments. "Yes!" she said a bit too loud, drawing the CHP officer's attention. "When do I start?"

"The grand opening is scheduled for the end of next month. So you're going to be very busy for the next five weeks."

"Bring it on! Where is it located? What's the square footage? Will the menu be the same? What about—"

"Whoa, girl. I know tomorrow's your day off, but let's sit down around four for an hour and go through the details."

"I'll be here." Elisa hugged Keith. "And thank you. Thank you for believing in me." Keith smiled, looking like a proud big brother.

"You've earned it. See you tomorrow, kid."

As Elisa crossed the parking lot to her car, she felt bolts of excitement shooting around inside her. A move to Folsom. A new diner. New responsibilities. A new life. She was ready!

Mario

Thursday, April 24, 2014

By the time Mario finished reading *Kipps* it was after midnight. He couldn't remember the last time he had wanted to finish an entire book in a single day.

Although he was beginning to drag from the long day and the late hour, he felt frozen to the sofa in his Lotus home, a rental he occupied while his house was under construction. The orange embers in the fireplace waved like a lava fountain and held him in a hypnotic state. It was eerie how much Arthur Kipps's life resembled his own.

Kipps had grown up poor, then inherited money and land, which changed his lifestyle and the way he thought of himself. Mario, whose mother had died in childbirth, became an orphan at the age of five when his father was killed in a farm accident at a Napa Valley winery. Aunts, uncles and cousins, who were also farm workers like his parents, provided food and a roof over his head for the next twelve years, but they could afford nothing else. He quickly learned to depend on himself and trust his instincts when life got tough.

The summer he turned seventeen also marked his graduation from high school. He was finally free to leave the fields that gave him a trapped and lifeless feeling. All his life he had heard (mostly from uncles when they drank too much) wild stories about his maternal grandfather who still lived in Mexico. So, a few weeks later, he packed everything he owned into a backpack, kissed his family good-bye, and traveled south to Mexico to find the man who shared his name.

When he arrived in Oaxaca, the grandfather he had heard so much about, the man he could not wait to meet, had passed away a month earlier. The family had been looking for him because his grandfather had named him in his will. Suddenly, the kid who carried everything he owned in a pack on his back found himself with $100,000 and a piece of land in Lotus, California. It was a life-changing experience and Mario had no intention of wasting his grandfather's gift. He returned to Northern California to attend college, then law school. By the time he graduated, the money was gone, but by then he had a law degree and a job in a busy Sacramento law office. Once again it was up to him to support himself, and he did it with hard work and by relying on his instincts.

Mario thought of Jolene and marveled at how she had matched him with H. G. Wells's book and how she recognized his restlessness that day just by looking at him.

He was beginning to think the restlessness was stemmed from his on-again, off-again (mostly off) love life. He really did want to get married and have a family. It was important to him. To his amazement, he enjoyed reading about Kipps's romance with Ann. And if he were truly honest with himself, he would like to have someone like Ann in his life—someone to share the home he was building, someone to share his work with, someone to plan a future with.

He yawned and stretched his way off the sofa and into the bedroom. Love and marriage will come, he reassured himself. While still in his running pants and T-shirt, he dropped back onto the bed. He intended to lie there for only a minute, but in less than that, he fell sound asleep.

In the morning he showered and dressed for the office, then watched the stock market opening bell while he ate a sunny-side up egg and a piece of wheat toast with salted butter. He glanced at his cell phone and noticed Tracey had called when he was in the shower.

He listened to her voice mail. "Hi, boss. You received a call yesterday while you were in court; I forgot to put the message on your desk. Beth needs you to stop by the bank to fix a problem with a transaction that she helped you with yesterday. It sounds pretty urgent. I'm calling in case you want to stop there before you come into the office. See you later." Click.

Mario had no idea what Beth, the bank's branch manager, needed. Yesterday he made a few deposits and transferred funds to the checking account to cover payroll on Friday. What could have gone wrong? Although, he thought, yesterday morning his mind was definitely distracted. He may have missed something.

He finished breakfast, rinsed the dishes, and placed them in the dishwasher. While at the counter, he drank the last two swallows of orange juice in his glass. An image of Beth drifted into his mind. She sure looked nice yesterday. Then he realized that, on more than one occasion, he had sensed some connection with her. But in his normal busy way, he didn't pay much attention to it—until now. Maybe this was Beth's way of getting him into the bank again.

He had known her professionally for about a year. He had noticed that whenever he visited the bank, she would make an effort to help him before any of the bank tellers could greet him. He assumed she did this with all of her business customers. Was there another reason for it? Should he ask her out? Of course he should, he thought. Today.

He shut off the television, picked up his car keys and briefcase, and headed for the door. With a bit more bounce in his step than usual, he headed for his Porsche.

Elisa

Friday, April 25, 2014

Elisa woke early the next day, still feeling high about her job promotion. The opportunity Keith and Lucy had offered her was a huge relief. "Thank you," she said out loud, her voice echoing off the bedroom ceiling.

She could hardly wait to share the good news with Jolene and talk about the book she had given her. Elisa showered, dressed, grabbed the last piece of fruit in the bowl on the kitchen counter, and headed for the front door.

When she pulled into the driveway, she saw Jolene sitting in one of the rockers on the front porch. Feather, stretched out on the porch at the top of the stairs, leapt up and ran to meet her as she got out of the car. "Hey, Feather." The dog's entire back end swayed back and forth as he wagged his tail.

Jolene closed the book in her lap. "Good morning! Join me?" she asked as she leaned forward in the rocker.

"I'd love to." Elisa smiled and sat in the rocker next to Jolene. Between the two chairs, she noticed a small table topped with a tray that held a teapot and two cups. "Oh. I'm sorry. Were you expecting someone?" Elisa said.

"Just you, my dear," Jolene replied with a soft giggle. "I always put out an extra cup. It seems to attract visitors." Jolene poured tea into the cup and handed it to Elisa.

Elisa moved the cup to her lips. Her nose detected a peach-y smell. She sipped the hot tea slowly and carefully. "I came by to thank you for recommending *Where the Heart Is*. I finished it yesterday."

Jolene nodded, a knowing look in her eyes. "What did you think of it?"

Elisa hesitated, taking in everything about the woman next to her who seemed to know things about her.

"It was easy for me to relate to Novalee," Elisa said. Then speaking in a matter-of-fact way, she added, "A family is really more than just people you're related to, isn't it? Novalee created a whole new life for herself, with a group of people who cared for her and Americus."

Jolene's eyes brightened and a soft smile filled her face. She didn't speak but shifted to a more comfortable position in her chair and sipped her tea.

"I like that Novalee didn't let her troubles take her down. She's a gutsy girl."

"Indeed," Jolene said.

"Jeez, can you imagine!?" Elisa said, cradling her cup, "having a baby in Walmart!" They both laughed at the idea.

"What are your plans now, Elisa?" Jolene asked as she pushed her toe against the floor of the porch, causing her chair to rock gently.

Elisa's whole face lit up and she sat up abruptly in her chair. "You're not going to believe this. I have fantastic news. I'm moving to Folsom. The owners of Sutter Diner are opening another restaurant, and they've asked me to manage it for them."

"Well, congratulations. New opportunities can be very exciting, can't they? Who knows where this will lead you."

Elisa nodded. "Yes. I think it's also time to end the empty relationship I have with Francisco, to make room for something new." This got an enthusiastic nod from Jolene.

Elisa's eyes softened and she set her cup down

on the tray. "Thank you, Jolene. For everything, but mostly for your friendship." She stood. "I have to go. If I had more time, I'd go inside and pick out a few books. You know I would. I'll come by and visit again before I move." She reached for Jolene and hugged her tightly.

"Trust yourself, dear," Jolene whispered in her ear.

Elisa waved from the car as she merged onto Lotus Road.

Mary June

Tuesday, April 29, 2014

When Mary June checked in at the Hartsfield-Jackson Atlanta Airport, the flight attendant at the departure desk (who appeared to be near the end of her work shift) forced a smile as she explained why the flight from Atlanta to Sacramento was delayed more than an hour. "Chicago's been hit all day—thunderstorms, rain."

"But we're not flying anywhere near Chicago," Mary June said.

"Yes, of course, ma'am. It's causing a chain reaction. Problems there are causing delays at nearly every major airport."

Mary June searched the woman's face, saw her weary smile and the bags under her eyes, and decided to let it go. She thanked the woman and tucked her boarding pass into her carry-on bag.

Truthfully, it didn't matter to Mary June where she was physically, because she was too distracted to be anywhere except in her head. The details of the last five days in Laurel continued to replay in her mind—conversations, childhood memories about the ranch that she had forgotten, her new relationship with her father.

Before anyone woke the first morning in Laurel, she walked around the grounds of the family homestead to see what had changed during her absence. Very little, she discovered. The family garden, freshly tilled the day before and now ready for vegetable seedlings from the greenhouse, passed a loamy smell that reminded her of the fun she and her brothers had had during planting season.

Not far from the garden, down a slope and along a narrow dirt path, she could hear the horses blowing dust from their noses. It comforted her to know that all she most loved about the family ranch had not changed. These were the pieces of her childhood that had shaped and touched her deeply. They were what really mattered.

While the ranch showed no change, the people who lived there did. A remarkable gentleness had come over her father, who was no longer a prominent attorney. Mother had passed away from cancer more than a year ago. Her brothers lived nearby and had busy lives of their own.

Father was now alone on the ranch with Stella, his cook and housekeeper, and Billy, who helped him with the horses. "This is my home, June

Bug," he told her the day before her scheduled return flight to Sacramento. "I won't leave just because I'm old. I will die here, as Mother did." Mary June understood his attachment to the ranch. If she were in his shoes, she would want the same.

Her two brothers still showed no interest in the ranch, which caused her to wonder if her visit had changed the fate of the old family home. Father had hinted that perhaps she would inherit it when he passed. She secretly hoped that someday it would be a place she could share with June, her biological mother.

She moved to one of the chairs next to the airline departure desk where people were waiting to board a flight to LaGuardia Airport in New York. She needed a few minutes to organize the items in her handbag and carry-on bag, and think about what to do for the next hour.

Her eyes settled on an attractive, well-dressed black man, his hair mostly gray, who leaned confidently and easily against the back of one of the chairs across from her and a few feet down. He grinned as he patiently listened to the woeful stories of the teenage boy sitting next to him.

The boy went on and on about this kid and that girl and Miss So-and-So, while the old man nodded, smiled, or raised an eyebrow when it seemed appropriate. It was obvious to everyone but the boy (his grandson?) that he wasn't really listening. The man caught her watching and playfully rolled his eyes and nodded in the direction of the boy. She grinned and bowed her head slightly in confirmation as she thought about her own crazy chatter going on in her head. The old man winked and then laid his large hand on the boy's knee, squeezing it until the boy stopped talking. "Let's go for a walk," he said. He stood slowly, as if his body was stiff from sitting too long.

More than an hour later, Mary June heard the boarding announcement for her flight as she made her way down the corridor from the coffee shop. She slipped her Kindle into her bag and stood near the edge of the seating area in front of her gate. She scanned the crowd flying to Sacramento to see if she recognized anyone. She didn't. Yet she marveled at the number of people who had something so intimate in common with her—an Atlanta to Sacramento trip on the same day. Why were they here? Who did they visit? Are they traveling home to Sacramento or is Georgia their home? She watched and tried to guess the story of each person in line.

As she settled into her seat next to the window, she observed the cargo crew load the remaining bags onto the plane. A man's deep, slow

Southern voice pulled her away from the window. "These are our seats."

Mary June looked up to see the old man she had been watching earlier. His teenage travel companion busied himself with getting comfortable in the aisle seat.

After they had settled next to her, Mary June held out her hand. "I'm Mary June. Nice to meet you."

The man took her hand gently. "My name is Jack. My grandson has been visiting me here in Atlanta." He glanced toward the boy whose head bobbed to the sound coming from the ear buds he wore. The old man shook his head. "His name is Jack, too. He lives in Sacramento, with his mother, my daughter. I've decided to stay with them a few days."

Mary June thought what a crazy coincidence to end up sitting next to the one person in the busy airport who had caught her attention.

"Is this your first visit to Sacramento?"

"Yes, ma'am." A concerned look crossed his face. "This is my first trip out of Georgia." He shrugged and looked out the window. "I've never had a reason to leave."

Mary June nodded. Few people stray far from where they grow up. Except, she had discovered, people who live in California. There, nearly everyone is from somewhere else. The plane started to pull away from the terminal.

As the plane took off, Mary June noticed Jack's left sleeve had crept up his arm to show a large burn scar that covered most of his left hand and forearm. She gripped both armrests as the plane ascended. "How are you on planes?" she asked.

He was rubbing his left arm, as if it ached, noticing Mary June's glances at his scar. "I'll let you know," he said. He nodded at his arm. "This old wound itches when I'm nervous."

The plane leveled into a smooth, even glide. "A bad house fire?"

"A bad kitchen fire—when I was eighteen." He was now rubbing the back of his hand. "This old scar is nothing. I lost my mama in that fire."

Mary June wanted to kick herself for being so nosy. "I'm so sorry."

Jack's voice was softer now. "Me, too. Everyone loved her. She'd do anything for anyone." He sighed. "I was on my own after that." He looked over at Jack #2 who looked like he didn't have a care in the world—his head on the headrest, his eyes closed, bopping to the music. "The kid here doesn't realize how lucky he is to have his mom."

Mary June paused and thought about how nice it would be to live with June at the family ranch, if the opportunity ever presented itself.

By the time Mary June arrived in Sacramento, picked up her bags, and exchanged hugs and contact information with Jack #1, it was after five in the evening. Somewhere over Colorado, she started to piece together the events that had taken place over the last week and realized these events had changed her whole life. While individually the events looked like coincidences, together they were not coincidences at all, and they certainly didn't feel like coincidences. And to think, it all started with Lotus's new bookstore owner, Jolene.

If traffic was light, Mary June figured she could make it home before the bookstore closed at seven. She had finished reading *Travels with Charley* before leaving Sacramento, and wanted to talk to Jolene about the book.

She pulled her car into the bookstore parking area and grabbed her purse from the passenger's seat. The late-April evening was warmer than usual, so Jolene had the front door fully open and latched to the wall. At the bottom of the stairs Feather greeted her with such an enthusiastic wag of his tail that his whole body swayed from side to side. "Hello, boy," Mary June cooed, scratching behind his left ear. "I missed you, too." She looked up when she heard Jolene's voice.

"Well, my stars! If it isn't Mary June," Jolene sang from inside the bookstore. "Where have you been? I was expecting you a few days ago to talk about that Steinbeck book." Jolene held Mary June's gaze and smiled, as if she knew exactly where she had been for the past few days.

"I've been in Georgia."

"Rediscovering your Southern roots?" Jolene said with a wink. "How about some tea? Today's blend has just a hint of peach flavor, to remind a person how easy it is to miss Georgia if you let yourself." Jolene didn't wait for Mary June's answer. She strolled over to the table next to her desk where a tea service tray sat, then poured two cups of tea.

Mary June helped herself to one of the cups. "Thank you."

"Let's sit a minute on the porch. Tell me all about your trip home."

Talking to Jolene was like talking to a friend

she had known her whole life. Mary June gave her all the highlights, including meeting her new friend, Jack, in the airport.

Then Mary June remembered the book. "By the way—"

"Yes, darlin'."

"How did you know I needed that book— *Travels with Charley*? I had been thinking about going back to Laurel for almost a year, but I wasn't sure it was the right thing to do until I got halfway through that story. I would have never picked it out on my own, but you gave it to me as if you *knew* it would give me a push."

"It was just a lucky guess," she said. "Did your Southern grandmother ever teach you to read tea leaves?" She swallowed the last of her tea and looked in the cup. "Hmm. Looks like travel's in my future." She turned to Mary June. "Drink up, darlin'. Let's see what your leaves have to say."

Mario

Wednesday, April 30, 2014

Mario enjoyed the light, joyful feeling that radiated from the center of his body as he watched Beth explain her decorating ideas for his new house. Fully animated, she tugged at invisible rugs, rubbed her hand over smooth hardwood floors, and swept her arms apart as she described the window coverings. It was clear by the look on her face that she was looking at a finished room. He liked that she wanted to be part of the process, since construction on his new house on the land his grandfather had given him would consume a lot of his time for the next six months. He listened and followed her as she bounced from room to room. Clearly, an interior decorator lay trapped inside this bank manager. Getting to know Beth over the past few days had been better than he had expected; he liked a lot about her.

A half hour later he pulled into the parking lot of the bank where Beth worked, behind a Cadillac that was moving toward the drive-up ATM. Beth leaned over and kissed him on the cheek. "Thank you for lunch. And the tour of your new home. It's very exciting."

Mario grinned. "You're welcome. After all that great decorating advice, I might owe you dinner."

"I hope I wasn't too pushy," Beth said, her face suddenly flushed. "I can't help myself."

"No, no. You helped me with more than a few decisions. I didn't realize building a house would require so much decision making."

Beth closed the passenger car door and bent to look into the open window, smiling. "See you tonight?"

"How about dinner at my house? I have a client coming in at five. Is six thirty okay? I'll grill the steaks."

"Perfect. I'll bring a salad." Beth waved and walked into the bank.

Before pulling the car onto Gold Hill Road, Mario glanced behind the passenger bucket seat to be sure Beth had not forgotten her lunch doggie bag and noticed H. G. Wells's book tucked inside the mesh pocket on the side panel. It had been a week since Jolene at The Hermit Bookstore had recommended *Kipps* to him. The day after he read it, he put it in the car as a reminder to stop and thank her.

He drove east toward the bookstore. When he

arrived, he saw Feather lounging on the front porch with his paws tucked under his mouth. The dog jumped up and greeted Mario like an old friend. "Hello, Feather. Where's Jolene?" Feather barked one loud bark and bolted toward the back of the store.

"Who's here, Feather?" Jolene said from behind one of the tall bookshelves.

"It's me, Jolene. Mario Pico." A long bohemian-style skirt waved at him from behind the bookshelf, then Jolene's face appeared.

"Mario! It's good to see you. How did you enjoy that wonderful book by H. G. Wells?" A sly smile formed on her face.

"As a matter of fact, that's why I'm here. I want to thank you for recommending the book."

"Oh, my pleasure. Was it what you needed?"

Mario laughed. "Yes, it was, more than you know."

Jolene bent down to grab a box of books. It looked heavy, so Mario reached for it and placed it on the cart behind her.

"Thank you." She rubbed her left hand as if it ached. "I'm glad you came by. I could use a break. Let's sit for a few minutes and you can tell me what you liked about *Kipps*." She laced her arm through his and directed him toward the antique velvet settee next to the fireplace.

"You know," Mario said as they sat down, "Arthur Kipps was someone I could really relate to, someone who had sudden wealth after having nothing, the loss of his parents, and then eventually choosing a life that was true to who he was." Mario paused. "H. G. Wells implied that none of the events that happened to Kipps were a coincidence. I can relate to that, too."

Jolene listened and nodded. "Yes, it's true. Mr. Kipps gets everything he wants once he's honest with himself."

Mario played with the keys in his hands and then looked up at Jolene, making eye contact. "Jolene, the morning I met you I was feeling unusually distracted . . . restless. I thought maybe you picked up on this, which is why you recommended the book."

Jolene's eyes lit up and she smiled. "Books often inspire action, especially if you acknowledge what you instinctively know you need."

Mario nodded. "But how did you know to give me *that* book?" He looked around at the shelves. "There's got to be hundreds of books in here."

Jolene shrugged.

"I would have never selected it on my own. You said you were certain it would help me."

Jolene glanced out the window. "I guess it's a little skill I've picked up over the years."

"Well, that's some talent." Mario stood, then helped Jolene up. "Thank you."

Jolene took Mario's arm and walked him toward the front door. "Do you have time to look around?"

"I wish I did, but I have to get back to the office. I'll stop by next week."

At the bottom of the front porch stairs, Feather sat waiting and thumping his tail. Mario bent down and scratched him behind the ear, then watched Jolene settle into one of the rocking chairs. *She'll be a good friend,* he thought as he waved and got into his car.

The Hermit Bookstore

Thursday, May 1, 2014

A steady spring rain fell in Lotus most of the morning, which kept Mary June tethered to the comfort of her apartment. She wrote poems in her journal and watched the rain stream off the shiny, bright-green oak leaves on the tree outside her living room window. It was a lazy Thursday and her day off. Just past midday she noticed the rain had stopped and the clouds had moved east, revealing a soft spring sun that had been there the whole time.

She lifted herself from the couch and stretched the ache in her lower back that took root whenever she sat too much. From the corner of her eye she caught a glimpse of the front cover of *Travels with Charley*. A picture of The Hermit Bookstore appeared behind her eyes. She checked the time, then grabbed her handbag, car keys, and the navy jean jacket hanging on the back of the chair in the kitchen.

When she reached Main Street, she slowed the Honda Civic to twenty-five miles per hour while a breeze carrying the fresh honey smell of eucalyptus pushed its way through the open passenger window. She inhaled the glorious smell and glanced at the

grove of giant eucalyptus on the right side of the road.
This was her usual route, yet she seldom noticed the
trees—either a symptom that she'd been in Lotus too
long or she wasn't living in the moment (maybe both).
She sighed. What else had she missed that had been
right in front of her all the time?

She braked as the stoplight turned from
yellow to red. Then she remembered a conversation
she had had with Russell, her eighty-something-year-
old neighbor. He said Australians brought the
eucalyptus to Lotus during the California gold rush,
and now, here they stood—sixteen decades later—tall
thickets that still perfumed the warm air after a good
rain.

She turned onto Lotus Road and followed the
curve to the bookstore. As she approached the old
farmhouse, she knew immediately something was
different. The exterior didn't have the same
welcoming aura that it had had on her last two visits;
it looked worn and tired.

She pulled the car into the parking space
closest to the front of the house and turned off the
ignition. The window shades on the parlor level and
the floor above it were pulled down. The porch chairs
where she and Jolene had talked and sipped tea two
days ago were gone. Debris from the surrounding
trees littered the floor of the porch, as if it had been

swirling around for months. There, once again, was the same vacant, quiet farmhouse that she had seen before the bookstore opened.

Then off to her left she noticed a rusty metal For Sale sign in the yard near the road. "What the hell?" she whispered. She got out of the car and stood staring at the house, feeling a little dizzy. Then she walked along the side, careful not to get too close. *This can't be. What's going on?* She reached for her phone and started taking pictures. The photos confirmed what she was seeing—and it wasn't Jolene's bookstore. She'd been here twice, she reminded herself, and had talked to Jolene both times. Then she remembered Elisa had also met Jolene.

When Mary June arrived at Sutter Diner, she took a seat at the counter. Thankfully the seats were empty except for the two stools at the opposite ends of the counter. Elisa set a cup of coffee in front of her and said, "What's wrong?"

"I have to talk to you," Mary June said in a hushed voice, wrapping her hands tightly around the cup. "I'm going crazy!"

"What are you talking about? And why are you whispering?"

Mary June swiped the screen of her phone and tapped until she found what she was looking for.

"Look!" she said, handing Elisa her phone.

"Okay. Old pictures of the farmhouse." Elisa shrugged.

"No, not old pictures. It's the farmhouse a few *minutes* ago." Mary June's eyes widened. "Look at the date and time. I took those ten minutes ago."

Mary June watched Elisa's eyebrows arch as she looked at the photos again. "I don't understand. Does this mean the bookstore's gone?" She looked disappointed.

"Yes, it's gone." Mary June said, annoyed. "But there's something else."

Elisa frowned. "What?"

"It looked as if no one had been there in months. Jolene couldn't have just moved out. And the For Sale sign is there again."

Elisa swept the air in front of Mary June with her free hand and turned around to set the coffee pot on its warming burner. "You *are* going crazy, girl. Of course Jolene was there. You told me about the book she gave you, and I talked to her a few days ago. I still have the books she gave me."

Elisa paused, thinking. "Wait! Mario bought a book there, too. He was in the diner yesterday. He asked if I'd been to the bookstore." She picked up the phone and looked at the photos again. "Can I use your phone to call Mario?"

"Of course."

Elisa pressed a few buttons and set the phone on the counter. "Pico Law Office," said a voice from the phone's speaker.

"Hey, Tracey. It's Elisa and Mary June at the diner. Is Mario available?"

"Hi, ladies. Yes, he's here. Let me connect you."

Mario's voice lifted from the phone. "Okay, something's wrong."

Mary June and Elisa looked at each other. "That's what we're trying to figure out," Elisa said. "Can you meet us at The Hermit Bookstore? It's important."

"Well, . . . sure, I can be there in a few minutes. Are you both okay?"

"We're fine. We'll see you in a few minutes. Bye." Mary June tapped the phone, ending the call.

Mario's Porsche was parked on the side of the farmhouse when Mary June and Elisa pulled into the driveway, but he wasn't in the car.

In a hushed voice Mary June heard Elisa say, "Oh my God." She was looking at the For Sale sign at the edge of the yard near the road. They got out of the car and walked toward the front porch. That's when they saw Mario walking from behind the house toward the parking area.

"What's going on?" he asked when he reached the front stairs. "Where's the bookstore?"

"Good question," Mary June said, climbing the stairs. Now that she had two other witnesses to protect her from whatever was going on, she felt slightly more confident about approaching the house. She stood on her toes and looked through the three small windows cut into the locked front door. They were lined with a layer of dirt, which she rubbed away so she could see the front parlor.

"What do you see?" Elisa asked.

She couldn't see anything except dirt and dust and old wooden furniture scattered about. "It's empty. It looks like nobody's been here in months, probably since last summer." She backed away from the door and inspected the porch. The floor was worn and dirty with old dry leaves blown into the corners.

Elisa searched for clues of a wooden post

where the bookstore sign had hung. Not only was there no post, there was no hole where a post might have been. "Where's the bookstore sign? It wasn't something you could just lift out of the ground and walk off with," she said.

"And why are the windows dirty?" Mary June said. "The porch looks like no one has walked on it in months."

Mario and Elisa looked at each other, silent. "There's got to be an explanation," he finally said with his brow wrinkled and his arms folded across his chest. He reached into his jacket and pulled out his cell phone. "I know the owner. He lives in Sacramento." He scrolled through the contact list in his phone. "Late last summer he came by my office and asked if I'd keep an eye on the place for him. Maybe I can get him on the phone." He tapped the screen twice, and after only one ring a man answered.

"Hello?"

"Cole. It's Mario Pico in Lotus."

"Mario. This is a surprise." He paused. "Is everything okay with the farmhouse?"

"Well, it looks that way. I'm here at the house with Elisa Evans and Mary June Shaw."

"Hi, Elisa. Hi, Mary June."

"Hi. Hello," they replied simultaneously.

Mario continued. "We're calling about the owner of the bookstore—the woman who rented the farmhouse. We came by today and she was gone."

"Did you say bookstore?"

"Yes."

"Mario, I don't know what you're talking about. The farmhouse should be empty. I didn't rent it to anyone."

Mario's eyes narrowed as he looked at Elisa and Mary June. No one said a word.

"I have books from the bookstore," Elisa finally said.

"So do I," Mary June confirmed.

"I do, too," Mario said.

"Maybe I should come by and look around." Cole's voice conveyed concern.

"The place is fine. It's secure," Mario said. "But there was a bookstore here yesterday, and I talked to the owner, Jolene."

"Did you say Jolene?" Cole asked. "I remember reading about a Jolene Fields."

Mario heard Mary June gasp. When he looked up, Mary June's and Elisa's expressions showed the same relief that he was feeling.

"Yes!" Elisa said. "That's her. Jolene Fields. She had a dog named Feather."

"The name of the bookstore, was it The Hermit Bookstore?" Cole asked.

"It was," Mario said, now feeling more relief. He knew there was a logical explanation. "It's the same owner and bookstore. Do you remember renting the place to her?"

"I never met her," Cole replied. "Last summer I saw her name and the name of the bookstore in a stack of papers in the old desk in one of the back bedrooms. As far as I could tell from the papers, she rented the place in 1964."

"Fifty years ago?" Mary June said, almost shouting, as she looked at Elisa.

"It sounds like the same person," Cole said. "I remember one more thing. A newspaper article in the folder with the rental application announced the bookstore's grand opening. In front of the farmhouse was an unusual sign—a large wooden thing with a carved picture of The Hermit from a tarot deck. You know, the man with the lantern. Like the one on Led Zeppelin's *Stairway to Heaven* album cover."

There was no doubt that Cole was talking about the same bookstore. A long pause followed as they tried to make sense of everything.

"Well, I don't know what happened," Mario finally said, "but the farmhouse is safe. You don't need to come, unless you want to."

"I appreciate you keeping an eye on it for me, Mario."

"I'm happy to help." Mario wanted to end the conversation. There was nothing more to say without alarming Cole. "I'll call you if anything comes up."

"Thanks. I already have a tenant lined up for this summer. He's scheduled to move in next month, to get the place ready."

"All right. Hope to see you soon, Cole. Bye."

"Bye," Cole replied. Mario tapped his phone.

Mario, Elisa, and Mary June turned to look at the farmhouse. No one spoke.

"What's going on?" Elisa said. "We all talked

to Jolene. We didn't dream up the bookstore. We all have books she gave us—books that were chosen by her for us."

"I can't explain it," Mario said softly, "but it happened."

"You have to admit," Elisa said, "there was something strange about how the bookstore appeared out of no where, and the way Jolene looked you in the eyes, as if she was searching for something." Elisa watched Mary June, who was being unusually quiet. "Are you all right?"

Mary June smiled. "I'm fine. I think what we experienced, y'all, was a little help from someone on the other side." Her chest softened as she thought about it. She felt humbled to have had the experience.

"There's no denying what happened to us," Mary June continued. "Cole just confirmed her bookstore was here in 1964, so she was definitely here." She paused and then her eyes lit up. "Just think of the effort that must have gone into helping us. If it had not been for Jolene's help, who knows when I would have returned to Georgia. It was time. I just needed a push."

Elisa and Mario nodded in agreement. They had needed Jolene's help as well.

"If you had come to me with a story like this," Elisa said, referring to Mary June, "I would've never believed you." She held her belly as she laughed away the last bit of doubt of their experience.

"Well," Mario said, "at least I have you both as witnesses. It didn't just happen to me." He turned to look at the For Sale sign. "If it had been just me, I would have wondered about my sanity."

Mary June giggled. "You're not crazy, my friend. When you need a little help, who cares where it comes from. Just be grateful, so it keeps on coming."

Excerpt from *The Medium*

The Medium
Copyright © 2015 by Linda Westphal

When tragedy visits you and delivers something unimaginable, the circumstances have a way of opening your heart and soul like you can't imagine. I know this to be true because eight months ago tragedy visited me.

On this Thursday afternoon in October, the air outside unusually crisp and still, I'm sitting on a plum-colored velvet sofa in Savannah's historic district.

While the exterior of the building has not changed in over 160 years, the interior has been remodeled and office suites now occupy the rooms.

A delicate scent (rose?) dances in my direction more than once as I take in the details of Caroline's office, which had once been the home's library. Decorated in a traditional Southern style, the room is as comforting as a big warm Southern hug. Even so, I'm a bundle of nerves about being here—in the office of a medium.

Caroline is not a stranger to me. A mutual friend formally introduced us in 2008, and over the years we've been invited to many of the same Savannah dinner parties. She is highly admired and respected in Savannah (as well as all over the world, I hear) for her ability to communicate with those who have passed on. Yet I've never felt inclined, until recently, to seek her assistance.

My hands in my lap are shaking. I take a slow, deep breath in and let it out even slower, forcing myself to relax. *What if no one comes forward to speak to me today?* I wonder. It is certainly possible. I close my eyes and focus on my breathing and the floral scent that hangs in the room. A moment later I hear the distant sound of heels hitting the wooden floor. I listen, my eyes still closed, as the sound gets closer and closer to the room where I am sitting.

When I hear the tall, wooden French doors open, I look in their direction and watch Caroline enter, her heels still clapping against the floor.

"Hello, Lacy," she says, her face gentle and her eyes wide and bright. She stops for a brief second and holds my gaze. All I can do is give her a weary smile. "Thank you for waiting." She turns and closes the doors, then settles in the Queen Anne chair next to the velvet sofa where I'm sitting. "Don't be afraid," she says. "All is well."

I brush an imaginary wisp of hair off my forehead and try to say something, anything, but nothing comes out. Again, I tell myself to relax, to trust Caroline and enjoy the experience.

She picks up a brilliant rough-cut purple amethyst from the table next to her chair and warms it in her hand. "Is this your first experience with a medium?" she asks.

I nod and manage to answer, "Yes."

"Please don't give me any details about why you're here. Spirit will guide us and provide what you need."

Then she closes her eyes and appears to be using energy from the amethyst to tap into wherever she goes to hear messages from the other side.

To continue reading, order THE MEDIUM at LindaWestphal.com

About the Author

Linda Westphal has written professionally since 1990 and now spends most of her time writing stories. *The Hermit Bookstore* is her second work of fiction. Her first book, *The Medium*, is available wherever books are sold. Linda lives in Northern California.

Connect with Linda Westphal —

Subscribe to receive updates and details about giveaways at **LindaWestphal.com**

Twitter: @Author_Westphal

www.ingramcontent.com/pod-product-compliance
Lightning Source LLC
Chambersburg PA
CBHW050425110726
47899CB00008B/2851